Taming Butterflies

Written by Sue Whiting

Illustrated by Mini Goss

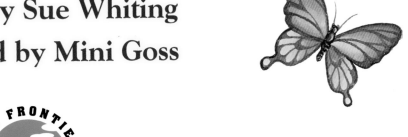

NEW FRONTIER PUBLISHING

To Lauren,
The first and bravest
Butterfly Tamer of all.
S.W.

For Hazel.
M.G.

First published in Australia in 2004
by New Frontier Publishing
ABN 25 192 683 466
6 Merle Street, Epping NSW 2121 Australia
www.newfrontier.com.au
Text copyright © 2004 Sue Whiting
Illustrations copyright © 2004 Mini Goss

All rights reserved
National Library of Austalia
Cataloguing-in-Publication data:
Sue Whiting, 1960–.
Taming Butterflies.

ISBN 0 9750907 5 5

1. Juvenile fiction.
2. Butterflies – Juvenile fiction.
I. Goss, Mini. II. Title.

A823.3

Designed by Ronald Proft
Printed in Hong Kong

Tilly had butterflies: thousands of fluttery butterflies.

And they lived inside her tummy.

Sometimes they were calm and quiet — no bother at all.

Other times,
they'd flit and flutter

causing trouble galore.

They swooped and swirled and dipped and dived and tickled Tilly deep inside.

They made her shiver.

They made her shake.

Sometimes they made her cry.

And the only place where they would stop
was close by her mother's side.

That was until Marjory-Anne came to visit.

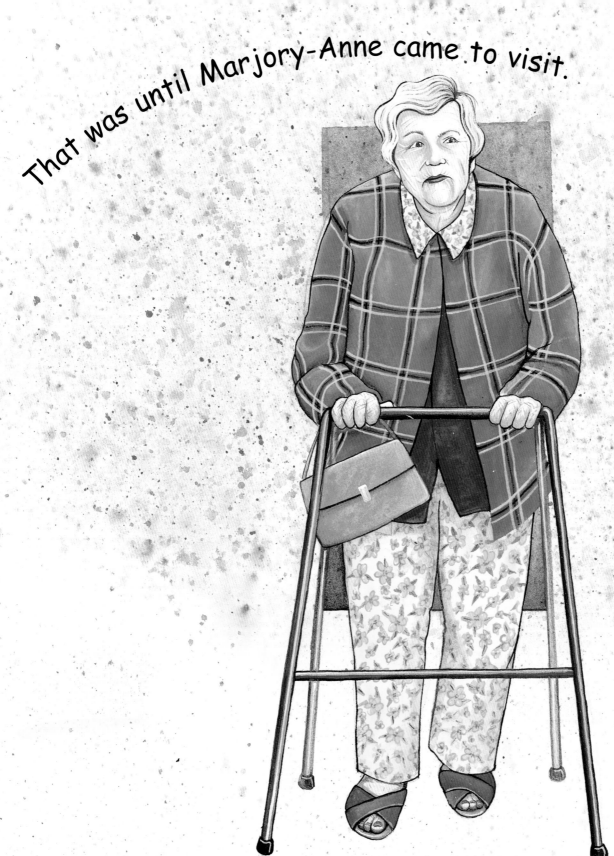

Marjory-Anne hobbled into the kitchen.

Her hair was silvery grey.

Her face was wrinkly, like someone had scribbled on it.

Clonk, clonk, clonk went Marjory-Anne's walking frame.

Tiny butterflies opened their wings.

"You must be Tilly,"
said Marjory-Anne.

Tilly's butterflies soared. They got stuck in her throat.

"Tilly's a bit shy," said Mum.
Marjory-Anne smiled.
Her eyes twinkled.

Tilly's butterflies looped the loop.

That night, Tilly snuggled in bed,
waiting for Mum's sweet dreams kiss.
Something clonked in the hall. *Clonk. Clonk. Clonk.*
Swish! Butterflies swirled and twirled.

Tilly dived under her doona.

"I've come to tuck you in, Tilly,"
Marjory-Anne said.

Tilly burrowed to the bottom of her bed.

"When I was your age, butterflies
gave me trouble too."
"They did?" said Tilly.

"They sure did. If you like, I'll teach you how to tame them."

Tilly crawled out from under her doona.
"Everyone has butterflies," continued Marjory-Anne.
"You have to teach them who's the boss.
Are they fluttering now?"
Tilly nodded.

"OK then," said Marjory-Anne. "Take a big breath."
Tilly frowned. How was that going to help?
"Come on," urged Marjory-Anne.

Tilly sucked in a deep breath.

"Now give your tummy a fierce stare,"
said Marjory-Anne. Tilly glared at her belly.

"You can be more fierce than that!" cried Marjory-Anne.

Tilly felt silly. She screwed up her
face and pushed out her lips.
She tried not to laugh.

"Next, tell your butterflies to be still!"

"Be still," said Tilly.

"Louder! Remember you're the boss."

"BE STILL!" Tilly shouted.

"Louder! Louder!"

"BE STILL!"

Tilly bellowed.

Tilly got the giggles. She giggled and giggled.
Marjory-Anne giggled too.
"How are your butterflies now?" she asked.
Tilly put her hands on her stomach.
"They've stopped!" she cried. "They're still."

"You did it, Tilly. You're a brave butterfly tamer."

Tilly threw her arms around Marjory-Anne's neck.

"Goodnight, Marjory-Anne."

"Goodnight, Brave Butterfly Tamer."

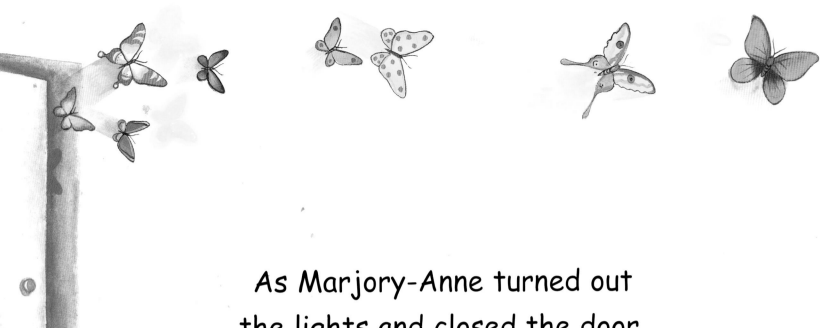

As Marjory-Anne turned out
the lights and closed the door,
from Tilly's room came an almighty roar,

"BE STILL, BUTTERFLIES!"

And they were.